Disney

Tutu Terrific!

By Kathy Ellen Davis
Illustrated by Vivien Wu

A GOLDEN BOOK • NEW YORK

randomhousekids.com
ISBN 978-0-7364-3504-8 (trade) — ISBN 978-0-7364-3505-5 (ebook)
Printed in the United States of America
10 9 8 7 6 5 4 3 2 1

One beautiful morning, the Palace Pets gathered in the Tutu Flower Fields to hear an announcement from Ms. Featherbon.

"Today is the Tutu Terrific Parade!" said the hummingbird. "All participants must create and wear a one-of-a-kind tutu that shows what makes them terrific. There's a table full of supplies for each of you. Have fun!"

The Palace Pets ran off to make their tutus.
All except Petite. The little pony furrowed her brow.
She didn't know what made her terrific. She decided
to ask her friends for help.

Petite trotted over to Berry, who was already almost done with her tutu. "Excuse me," Petite said to the bunny. "How do you know what you're terrific at?"

"Easy," replied Berry. "I'm terrific at this!" Her furry arms moved quickly as she grabbed berries and frosting . . .

. . . and created a yummy cupcake that looked just like the Pawlace!

"That's **amazing**!" Petite exclaimed.

Perhaps Petite was terrific at making treats, too.
The pony gave it a try, but she ended up making
a big mess instead. Food flew everywhere, and the
berry bowl landed on Berry's head!

"I guess treats aren't my thing," Petite said.
"But that bowl hat would be the perfect finishing
touch for your *berry* sweet tutu."
"You're right!" said Berry. "Thanks, Petite!"

Next Petite went to see Pumpkin. She was wearing a glamorous, glittery tutu—perfect for the puppy who was the best dresser. But something wasn't right. Pumpkin had lost an earring!

"Don't worry, Pumpkin," Petite said. "I've got an eye for earrings!" The helpful pony searched through the flowers and grass and found what her friend needed.

"Oh, thank you, Petite!" Pumpkin exclaimed.
She clipped the earring to her ear and twirled.

Petite was happy that she had been able to help
Pumpkin, but she still didn't know what made her
terrific. How would she make a tutu for the parade?

Petite trotted off to find Dreamy. The kitten was
hard at work sketching a tutu that resembled pajamas.
"Your tutu will be so nice and cozy," Petite told her.

Petite was just about to ask if Dreamy could help her figure out what made her terrific, when she heard snoring. Dreamy had fallen asleep!

She really is a terrific napper, Petite thought.

Petite didn't want to disturb her friend, but she was worried that Dreamy's tutu wouldn't be finished in time. So the helpful pony grabbed some supplies and got to work.

Dreamy was amazed to find her tutu finished when she woke up!

Not long after that, it was time for the parade.
"Places, everyone!" Ms. Featherbon called.
Petite knew she couldn't be in the parade. She didn't
have a tutu because she still didn't know what made her
terrific. She walked away with her head hanging low.

Berry, Pumpkin, and Dreamy didn't want Petite
to miss out on the parade.

"If it weren't for Petite," said Berry, "I wouldn't
have my pretty hat."

"And I wouldn't have my earring," said Pumpkin.

"And my tutu wouldn't be finished," said Dreamy.

The friends knew just what to do. They used pieces of their own tutus to make a new one for Petite!

Rip!

Tear!

Chomp!

Pumpkin found Petite wandering through the Tutu Flower Fields.

"I don't know what makes me terrific," the sad pony told Pumpkin.

"Well, *we* do," Pumpkin said. "Come with me!"

Petite couldn't believe her eyes.

"It's a friendship tutu!" Pumpkin, Berry, and Dreamy announced.

"Because you are the most terrific friend!" Berry added.

Petite smiled wide. "It's tutu terrific!" she exclaimed. "Thank you!"

Just then, Lily appeared with a tutu made of musical instruments. She got the parade started and led the way for her friends. Everyone marched grandly in their tutus . . .

. . . but Petite was the proudest!